Kenny's Amazing Adventures

By Anita Lynn Lee

Illustrated by Rosemarie Jackson

AuthorHouse™
1663 Liberty Drive
Bloomington, IN 47403
www.authorhouse.com
Phone: 1-800-839-8640

First published by AuthorHouse 9/18/2009

ISBN: 978-1-4490-1588-6 (sc)

Printed in the United States of America
Bloomington, Indiana

This book is printed on acid-free paper.

authorHOUSE®

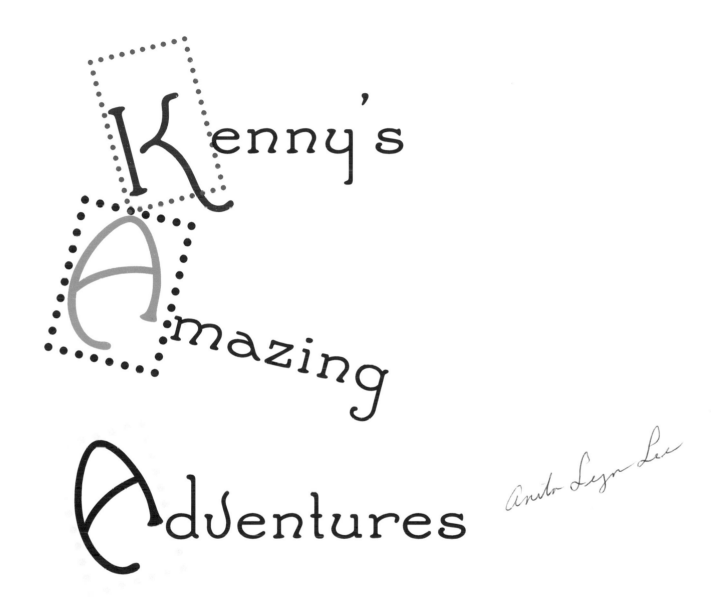

Kenny's Amazing Adventures

By Anita Lynn Lee

Illustrated by Rosemarie Jackson

Anita Lynn Lee

For Kenechi, Kamara, Emeka, Samuel, and Orlando

Acknowledgements:

Many thanks to my husband, mother and all of my family and friends

for support

Heartfelt thanks to my wonderful editor, long-time friend, and mentor, Marie Blake

Special thanks to my creative illustrator, Rosemarie Jackson

Thanks to those clever Shepherd students for their input and feedback

Special kudos to my imaginative grandson, Kenechi Chima, who enjoys life's adventures

Buddy

One morning as Kenny got out of his bed

He looked all around and he really felt scared.

His Buddy was gone.

He was missing you see.

Where on earth was his Buddy?

Oh, where could he be?

He thought about places where Buddy would hide.

Kenny knew in the past he could find him with pride.

At the foot of the bed

Snuggled under the sheet,

He'd been easy to spot

And Kenny thought that was neat.

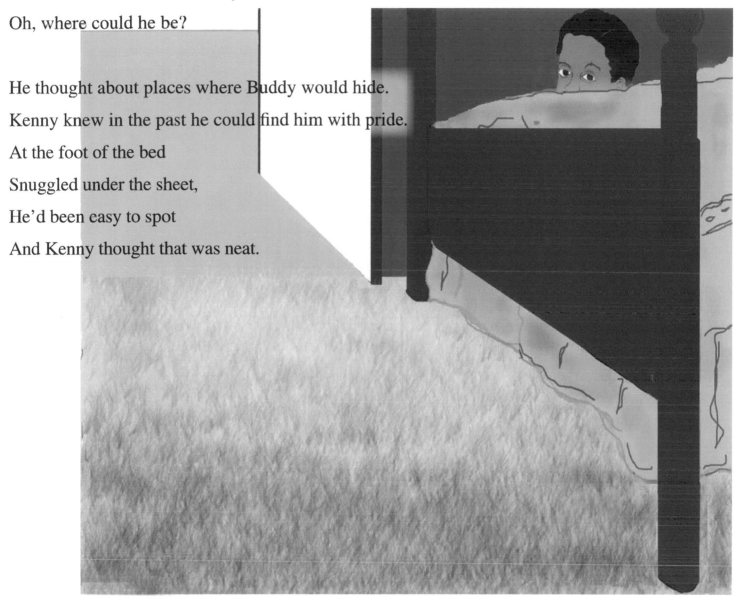

Buddy was not in his usual place.

Had he vanished through the night without even a trace?

He just was nowhere

As far as Kenny knew,

But he had to keep looking.

There must be a clue.

Then Kenny searched deep down under the bed.

Maybe Buddy had fallen and hurt his big head.

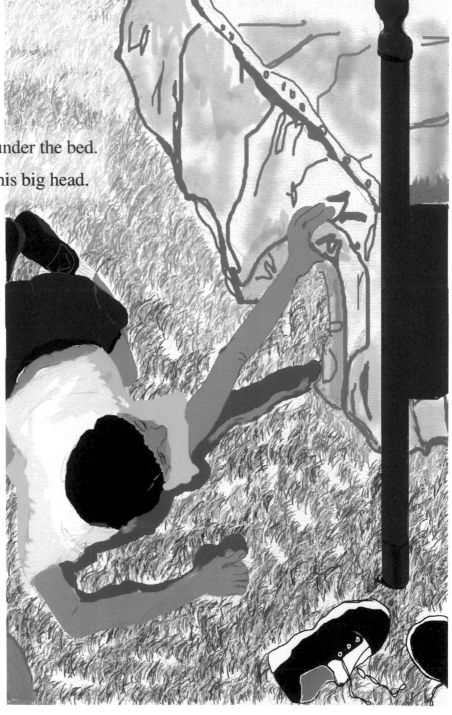

Kenny looked in his toy box

And on his bookshelf.

He was moving so fast

He was quite beside himself.

Now he was determined to hunt until night

For his little Buddy who had gone from his sight.

He rummaged through his closet

And each dresser drawer.

He even looked carefully

Behind every door.

He pulled out all of his stuffed bears and kittens.

He poked through coat pockets that had his new mittens.

He ran to the hallway

But no Buddy there.

.

He looked in the bathroom

In his big potty chair.

Because Kenny's search was ending up bad,

He plopped on the floor and he really felt sad.

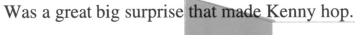

Suddenly from nowhere

Mom opened his door.

She brought his clean clothes

And she brought something more.

For there in the laundry basket sitting on top

Was a great big surprise that made Kenny hop.

His good old stuffed Buddy

Mom had washed too.

Now his fuzzy old pal

Smelled clean, fresh, and new.

So Kenny hugged mom and he hugged his stuffed friend.

He felt so delighted to have Buddy again.

He cleaned up his room

As best as he could.

Then he and Buddy

Were together for good.

People Don't Mean What They Say

Kenny tried to be good and follow directions but even when he did he sometimes got into trouble. He wondered why people didn't really mean what they said.

On Monday when Mom was making up Kenny's bed, he complained about the puzzle pieces his sister had scattered on his floor. Mom just looked at Kenny and asked, "Kenny, did you get up on the wrong side of the bed?" He didn't know which side of the bed was right and which was wrong. Then he looked at his hands and thought, left… right. Quickly he climbed back into the bed to get up on the right side, but mom frowned saying, "What's wrong with you? I just straightened your bed." Kenny felt sad because Mom couldn't see that he was following her directions. He figured that people just don't mean what they say.

On Tuesday when Kenny ran to the breakfast table, Dad said, "Watch your step or you'll fall." Immediately Kenny looked at each foot as he walked, but Dad commanded, "Hold your head up before you bump into something." Didn't dad realize how confusing it was following his directions? Kenny could see that people just don't mean what they say.

▲▲▲▲▲▲▲▲ ▲▲▲ ▲▲ ▲▲▲▲▲

On Wednesday Kenny and his big brother went to the doctor's office. As Kenny reached for the elevator button his brother cautioned, "Move back from that elevator door." So Kenny stepped backward to the wall behind him, but his brother shouted, "Come up here. The elevator door is opening." Had his brother forgotten his own directions? Obviously people just don't mean what they say.

On Thursday, Kenny's uncle took him to the theater.   As Uncle parked the car he said, "It's almost time for the movie to begin. You need to shake a leg." Kenny didn't understand why shaking his leg would help, but he sat there shaking it. Uncle looked upset and said, "Stop wasting time. Let's go." Didn't Uncle remember the directions he gave? Clearly people just don't mean what they say.

On Friday Grandma and Poppop came to visit. Kenny asked them, "Would you like to see my Noah's Ark collection?" Quickly, he ran upstairs to his room to get his toy animals. In an instant Kenny was back downstairs with his Noah's Ark collection.

Grandma said, "Hold your horses, young man. You don't have to hurry." So he slowly pulled both of his horses from the bag and stood there holding them.

Poppop chuckled, "Put down those horses. Let us see your entire collection."   Kenny guessed that Poppop didn't hear Grandma or maybe he already knew that people don't mean what they say.

On Saturday his family visited GG, his great-grandma. She kept leaving her cane in one room or another, but Kenny and his sister would bring it back to GG. Kenny wondered how GG managed when he and his sister were not around to help. When the family was leaving, G.G. whispered, "You know that I'm as blind as a bat. Cross your fingers that I might keep up with my own cane." Everyone but Kenny gave GG a good-bye kiss. He stood there with his fingers crossed. GG said, "Aren't you going to give me a kiss, Kenny?" He wondered if her blind bat eyes could see his fingers so that she would know that he had been following directions. Then, like always, he realized people just don't mean what they say.

On Sunday when the family went to a restaurant for breakfast, Kenny brought his donut and juice back to the car. Just as he sat down, everyone began to give him demands.

Mom told him, "Finish your donut and juice."

His brother added, "Kenny, roll down your window."

His sister begged, "Hand me my doll.

Then Dad insisted, "Buckle up so that we can take off."

Kenny had always tried to be polite and he didn't want to bite the hand that fed him but he figured that he was between a rock and a hard place when he blurted out, "Do you think I'm an octopus?" Everyone stopped and looked at him, but just for a moment. They already knew that people don't really mean what they say.

Super Kenny

Just call him Kenny in the middle. He was the middle child in his family between his bossy older brother and his attention-seeking younger sister. He was the middle child in his class picture because he was not very tall and not very short. Even his name, Kenny Machi, was in the middle of the alphabet so when things were given out in alphabetical order, he would not ever be the first to receive them. All day long Kenny was caught in the middle where he never felt special.

▲▲▲▲▲▲▲▲▲▲▲▲▲▲▲▲

Nighttime, though, was different. Just around dusk after Kenny had taken his bath and brushed his teeth he would put on his warm pajamas and grab his silky cape. Then he would climb into bed next to his Fuzzy Buddy, close his eyes, and dreamily become Super Kenny. Super Kenny always helped people when they were having problems and saved people when bad things happened. He was a hero at home, in school, and in his community.

One day when Kenny's sister was riding her tricycle in front of their house, he heard the neighborhood bully scoff at her, "Get off the sidewalk. You're in my way."

Kenny puckered up and blew so hard that the wind lifted that bully into the air and carried him back down the street. Every time that bully tried to walk forward he kept being blown back.

Kenny's sister said, "Thanks, Kenny, you surely are super."

Another time when his teacher was trying to place a big box onto the top shelf, she couldn't quite lift it there. Up went the box, back down it came. Up went the box, back down it came.

"Ha! Ha! Ha! Giggle, giggle!" laughed the children.

Kenny stretched out his arm so far that he nudged that box right up onto the shelf without even leaving his desk.

The teacher said, "Thanks, Kenny, you surely are super."

Recently, when Kenny was walking his dog, Snowball, the dog began barking at two girls who were riding their bikes. The girls got scared and ran right into the mail carrier whose mail scattered everywhere. The mail carrier stepped off the curb to pick up the mail just as a bus came along. In order not to hit the mail carrier the bus driver slammed on his breaks so quickly that a man who was standing on the bus almost fell into a lady's lap.

"Look out, Mister!" she snapped. "Didn't you see me sitting here?"

"Excuse me," the man apologized, "but it was the bus driver's fault." Then he turned to the bus driver and shouted, "Can't you drive this bus?"

"Excuse me," the bus driver apologized, "but it was the mail carrier's fault." The bus driver leaned out the window and yelled, "Mail Carrier, watch where you're going."

"Excuse me," the mail carrier apologized, "but it was those girls' fault." He shook his finger at the girls, scolding, "Stop running wild. You knocked the mail everywhere."

"Excuse me," each girl apologized, "but it was that dog's fault."

Kenny was sorry about the problems that his dog had caused. "Wheeeeew," Kenny whistled. Everyone stopped and looked at him. "Snowball, go home," Kenny commanded. Off went Snowball. Then, swoosh, swoosh, swoosh, here, there, everywhere as quick as lightning, he began picking up the mail from the street, sidewalk, and yards.

"Wow! Look at him go," said the mail carrier.

"Isn't he fast," said the two girls spellbound.

The bus driver, the lady and the man climbed down from the bus to watch Kenny in action. Kenny found the mail that had blown into bushes, under cars, and even behind buildings. It was so exciting that people in the neighborhood came out and clapped as Kenny collected the last bit of mail and handed it to the mail carrier. When Kenny had finished, the mail carrier said, "Thanks, Kenny."

Then everyone shouted, "You surely are super." The mail carrier said, "You are so super that we should call you Super Kenny."

Everyone agreed and shouted, "Super Kenny, Super Kenny!"

At night Super Kenny was in the midst of problems and always proved himself to be a hero at home, at school, and throughout the community. So now when Kenny awakens each morning he is glad to be in the middle of things because being in the middle makes him feel special.

LaVergne, TN USA
11 November 2009
163729LV00005B